Henry's First-Moon Birthday

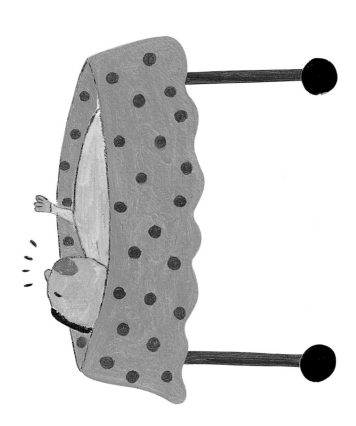

by Lenore Look   illustrated by Yumi Heo

AN ANNE SCHWARTZ BOOK   ATHENEUM BOOKS FOR YOUNG READERS
NEW YORK   LONDON   TORONTO   SYDNEY   SINGAPORE

For my elementary-school librarian, William C. Towner,
who has fed countless children parable and possibility, and in
whose library my journey began, *Many Moons ago.* —L. L.

To Aunt Melanie,
for her delicious apricot cookies
—Y. H.

ACKNOWLEDGMENT

Many thanks to Molly Hanessian, who made sure
Henry was properly dressed

GLOSSARY

first-moon birthday party: celebration at
the end of a baby's first month of life

GninGnin: paternal grandmother

mou-haur mou-noh: literally, "no head, no brain"; forgetfulness

YehYeh: paternal grandfather

Aiyaah!: oh no!

hungbau: a red envelope used for money gifts

gunghay: congratulations, good luck

Loong: boy's name, "dragon"

Lai Nor: girl's name, "graceful doe"

Baba: father

FIRST
EDITION

Atheneum Books for Young Readers
An imprint of Simon & Schuster Children's Publishing Division
1230 Avenue of the Americas
New York, New York 10020

Text copyright © 2001 by Lenore Look
Illustrations copyright © 2001 by Yumi Heo
Book design by Michael Nelson
The text of this book is set in ITC Highlander.
The illustrations are rendered in pencil, oil, and collage.

Printed in Hong Kong
10 9 8 6 5 4 3 2 1

Library of Congress Cataloging-in-Publication Data
Look, Lenore.
Henry's first-moon birthday / by Lenore Look;
illustrated by Yumi Heo. —1st ed.
p.   cm.   "An Anne Schwartz Book."
Summary: A young girl helps her grandmother with preparations for
the traditional Chinese celebration to welcome her new baby brother.
ISBN 0-689-82294-4
[1. Babies—Fiction. 2. Grandmothers—Fiction. 3. Chinese Americans—Fiction.
4. Brothers and Sisters—Fiction.] I. Heo, Yumi, ill. II. Title.
PZ7.L8682He   2000   [E]—dc21   98-21626

This is me, Jen, Jenny, but never Jennifer.
I am a.k.a. Older Sister, and I've been in charge of our house ever since Mother had a baby.

And this is GninGnin, but never Grandmother or Granny or Grandma.

She came to live with us, to help out, when Mother went to the hospital.

Tomorrow she goes home.

GninGnin makes everything with her hands: sweaters, blankets, noodles, Christmas ornaments, and the world's prettiest braids right in my hair.

This is the sun in my bedroom window as it slips in front of the stars, just as GninGnin and I slip out of bed. It is Baby Henry's one-month birthday, his first-moon, they call it in Chinese. If you ask me, his face is round as the moon, because all he does is eat—except when he's sleeping or crying. Anyway, there will be a big celebration for him, a first-moon birthday party, and we have a lot to do before everyone comes.

This is our kitchen, all ready for us to cook. There are mushrooms and dates and mysterious things floating in bowls. GninGnin touches this one here and that one there, like a gardener tending her plants. She fills our biggest pot with water enough for a bath.

This is what happens when the water boils. GninGnin gently slides a chicken into the bubbles. The chicken turns creamy white underneath its yellow skin. As I watch, my stomach growls like a bear and GninGnin exclaims, *"Mou-haur mou-noh! I forgot your breakfast!"*

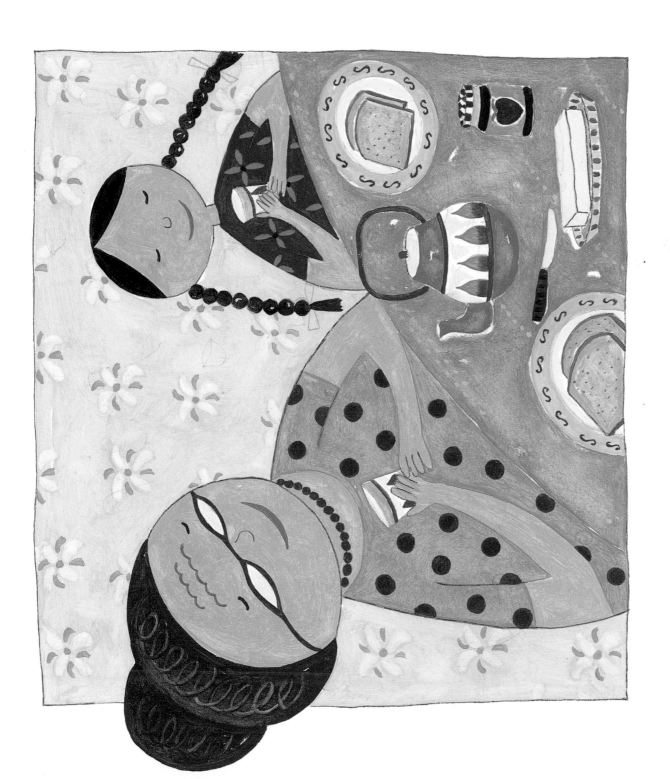

This is me and GninGnin, sitting for just a minute to eat our toast. GninGnin pours me hot tea that smells like flowers. I sip slowly to make it last, and also to keep from burning my tongue. GninGnin taught me this, and she is pleased that I remember.

This is ink, the real stuff, which GninGnin makes by rubbing an ink pebble with a little water. She holds my hand to write the baby's Chinese name, Loong, with a brush. It means *dragon*, and it looks like one too. My name, Lai Nor, means *graceful doe*, but it looks like a plain old goat—it isn't fair! GninGnin writes good-luck words on a red cloth for everyone to read.

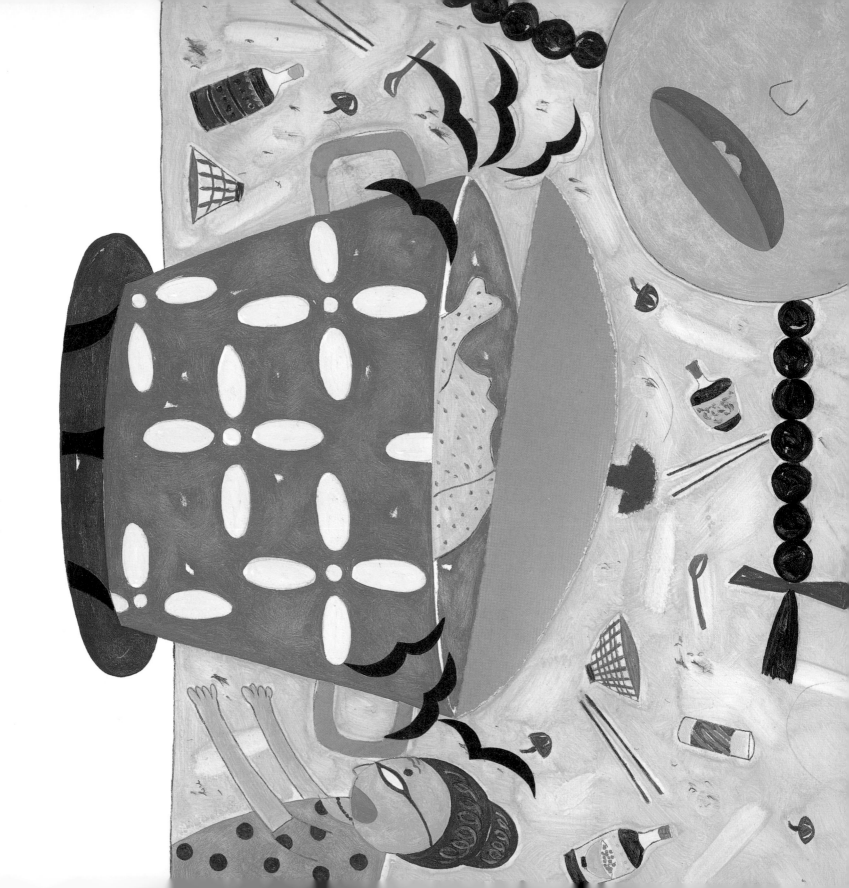

This is the chicken pot boiling over.

Look at GninGnin go! She turns down the heat. Her lips disappear. Her fingernails scrape off the warts on the wood fungus. *Chop, chop,* the mushroom feet fall off. She drops everything into the soup, one, two, three. I try to help, but GninGnin is too busy.

So I am busy too. Oops! This is ink, the real stuff, on the floor. I make it look like a spaceship, and then a dinosaur, and then . . . I make my escape. But GninGnin turns and sees. Her face becomes gray like a rainy day.

Here I am saying I'm sorry. GninGnin forgives me and
we hurry to clean the mess before Mother comes down.

This is GninGnin keeping an eye on me. Her face is pink again, like the salmon on crushed ice at the Pike Place Market. She starts the pigs' feet and ginger soup "to help Mother make milk for her baby," GninGnin says. "But good for everybody." I am in charge of the brown sugar. It's better than candy from the store. GninGnin pretends she doesn't see the sweet, sticky goo running down my chin. Yum!

This is Baba, Dad, Daddy, Pops, and Poppy. He answers to most anything. He usually doesn't look too good until he's had his coffee. He wraps his arms around me and nuzzles me with his quillery face. I remind him to pick up YehYeh, my grandpa, for the party.

"No problem, Captain," he says.

This is our car. Usually it is no problem. But today, if you look closely, you can see Father peeking out from underneath. And this is Mother, coming out to ask him to pick up Grandaunties Judith and Mei Lan, my favorites, who also need rides. "Aiyaah," Mother exclaims when she sees greasy smudges all over Father's good clothes.

Look at the clock! Time flies, and so does Mother. She cleans like a tornado going through every room. Uh-oh, look at the vase! Mother does a front two-and-a-half dive.

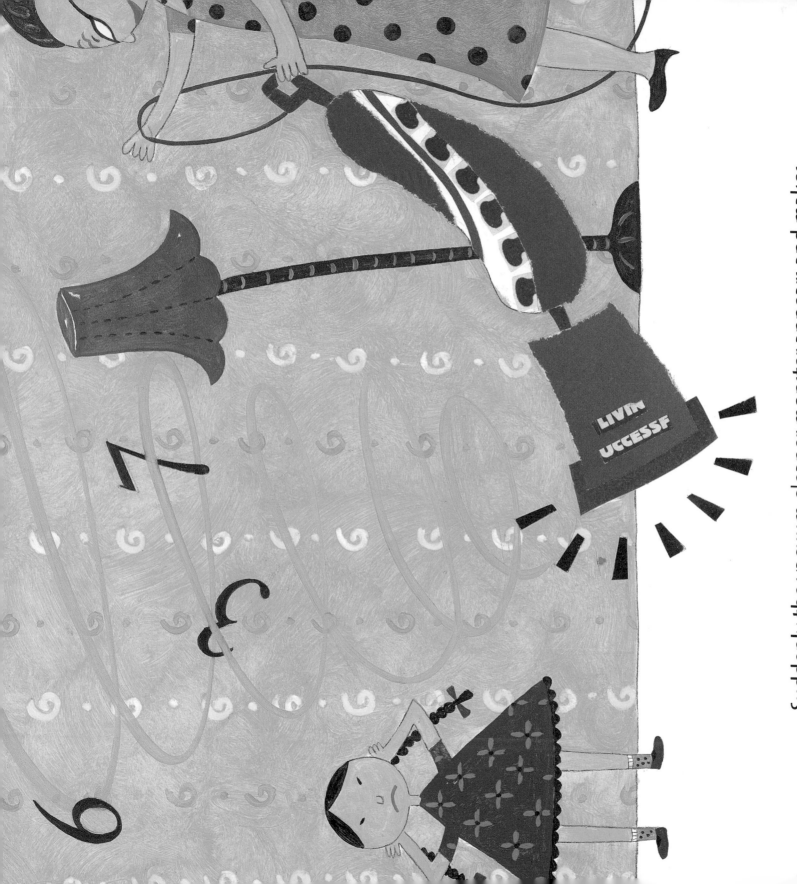

Suddenly the vacuum cleaner monster appears and makes

Baby Henry cry. "Waaaaah!" Mother runs to comfort him.

This is GninGnin and me working fast as machines. She boils a million eggs. She hands me a *hungbau* and shows me how to dip it into water to make the red dye come off. Then she rubs the hungbau all over an egg, turning it red. They are lucky eggs to welcome the baby. Look at silly me. Red as a firecracker.

This is my bath. GninGnin scrubs me clean as celery. I slip into a new dress and GninGnin makes new braids in my hair and ties on new ribbons.

GninGnin slips into an old dress that looks like new. "I wore this at your first-moon birthday," she says. "Special dress for special occasion." I look in the mirror and see that we are a pair, like favorite shoes, side by side.

This is our house, busy as King Street Station. The taxi arrives just in time with Father, YehYeh, and my grandaunties. Behind them come all our other relatives. Here is Uncle Ho. He is a cook, and he brings Mother a crate of oranges to wish her health and happiness.

And here is Uncle Peter. He is a mailman, but today he's just a regular guy. He pumps Father's hand up and down. "Gunghay! Gunghay!" he shouts, slapping a ton of good luck on my father's back.

I kiss Grandauntie Judith, who smells like old books—she works at the library. And Grandauntie Mei Lan, who smells like music—she teaches piano.

And this is Baby Henry, I almost forgot. He's tired from his first haircut. See the gold chain and coins around his neck and the hungbaus tucked into his blanket? Everyone says he looks like a fancy butterfly in his silky new clothes.

I don't just *look* like a butterfly, I can *fly* like one too, but no one notices. "What a good baby," they say.

I'm in charge of making sure the cousins don't wake Henry. I do a good job until—I can't resist—I pinch him once when no one's looking.

This is how to eat pigs' feet and ginger soup. My cousins and I spit out the knuckles and try to reconstruct the feet. When the grown-ups aren't around, we peek inside Baby Henry's hungbaus and count more than one hundred dollars! We think of a million great ways to spend it. Then we jump on the beds.

This is Mother thanking GninGnin for coming to take care of us, after everything has quieted down. Mother is sad, but I am sadder.

"JenJen was a big help," GninGnin says. "She was in charge of everything." I love it when she calls me that—JenJen sounds almost like GninGnin. But I am too tired to tell her. Maybe in the morning, when she is leaving and the whole world is about to change, I'll tell her. And someday, I'll tell Baby Henry that it was the best first-moon birthday party ever and that he was lucky to have me in charge.

And this is Baby Henry, smiling at me, his eyes like commas, he's so happy. I smile back, and—I can't help it—kiss him good night. For a baby, he really is very good. And that makes us a pair, like matching socks, side by side.

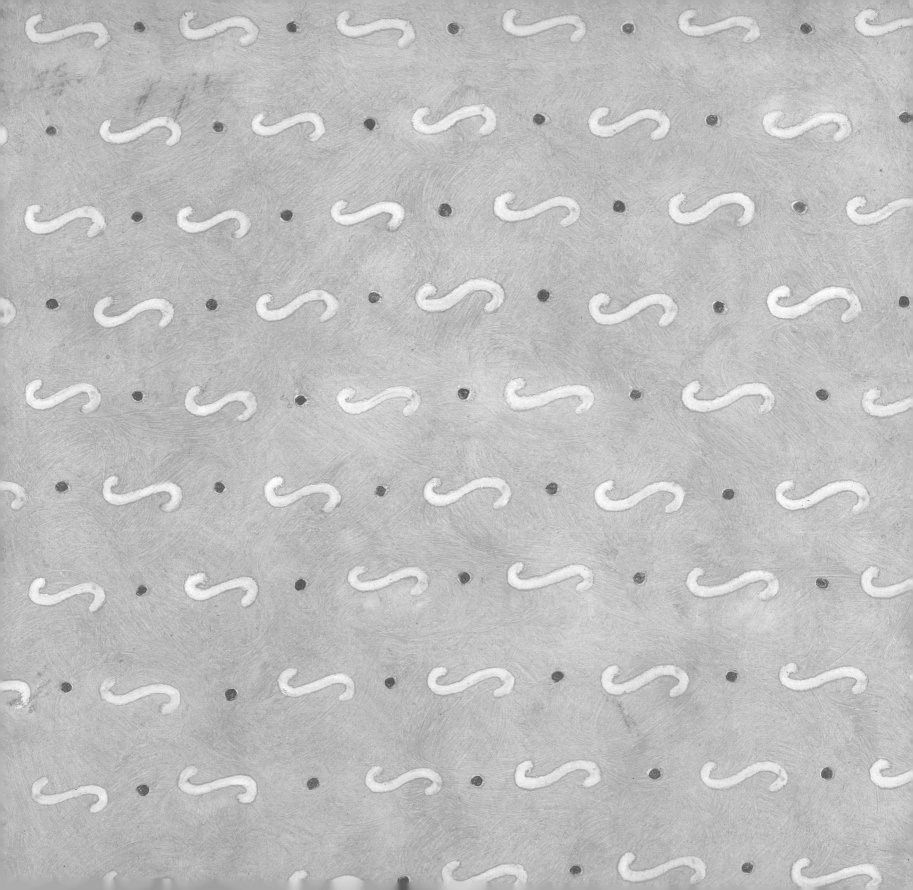